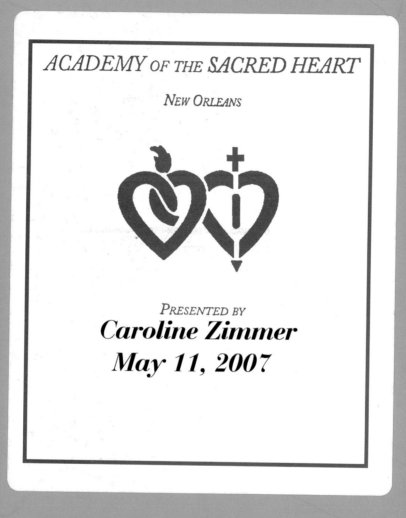

ACADEMY OF THE SACRED HEART

NEW ORLEANS

PRESENTED BY
Caroline Zimmer
May 11, 2007

The Socksnatchers

LORNA BALIAN

STAR BRIGHT BOOKS

NEW YORK

Published in the United States of America by Star Bright Books, Inc., New York.
The name Star Bright Books and the Star Bright Books logo are registered
trademarks of Star Bright Books, Inc. Please visit www.starbrightbooks.com.

ISBN 1-59572-003-0

Library of Congress Cataloging-in-Publication Data

Balian, Lorna.
   The Socksnatchers / by Lorna Balian.
      p. cm.
   Summary: Whenever a sock disappears in the Perkins household, the
Socksnatchers who live in the cellar unbeknownst to the family members,
are preparing a tasty meal.
   ISBN 1-59572-003-0
   [1. Socks--Fiction. 2. Humorous stories.] I. Title.

PZ7.B1978Sn 2005
[E]--dc22
                                                      2004029612
T 69023

Why is Mama Socksnatcher distressed?
    She's too upset to tell us right now.

Why is Papa Socksnatcher distressed?
    Because he feels so helpless when Mama cries.

Why is Abner Socksnatcher so miserable?
Because he knows he has done something wrong–again.

Why is Daisy Socksnatcher so smug?
    Because she knows SHE never does anything wrong–EVER.

Why is Mama Perkins so distressed?
   Because she's trying to match up socks–and they don't.

Why isn't Papa Perkins distressed?
   Because he's not home right now.

Why is Jason Perkins peeved?
　　Because he has to clean his room and look for missing socks.

Why is Mollie Perkins peeved?
　　Because she has to clean her room for the same reason.

Why is the cat acting so silly?

Because he's hearing strange noises in the cellar again.

"I've told him and told him!" wailed Mama Socksnatcher. "Snatching one sock is SHARING, but taking a pair of socks is STEALING! Abner has disgraced our family honor!"

"Calm down, Mama," muttered Papa. "He's just a child. He'll learn."

"But Papa! He stole a pair of CLEAN socks!" gloated Daisy.

"CLEAN socks!" yelled Papa. "What use are CLEAN socks? You'll have to return them!"

So, in the dead of night,
very quietly to avoid the cat,
Abner crept back through the sleeping house.
He returned the clean pair of socks,
but he couldn't find a single smelly sock anywhere.
The rooms had been cleaned!
Oh, woe! Disgrace heaped upon disgrace.

There was misery in the Socksnatcher hidey-hole. . .

Abner had to memorize the family rules. He was an outcast!

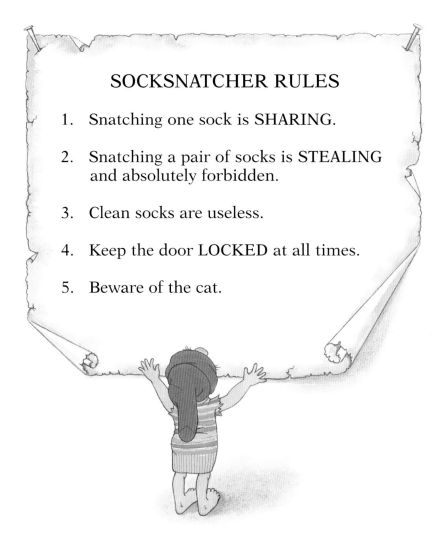

SOCKSNATCHER RULES

1. Snatching one sock is SHARING.

2. Snatching a pair of socks is STEALING and absolutely forbidden.

3. Clean socks are useless.

4. Keep the door LOCKED at all times.

5. Beware of the cat.

Mama couldn't cook soup without smelly socks–could she now?

Papa got awful ornery when he was hungry, of course.

Daisy kept reminding everyone that their pitiful situation
was all Abner's fault. SHE never did anything wrong!

Mama Perkins told Papa she'd just have to buy some new socks. "There aren't two socks that match in this whole pile!" she said.

"I see what you mean," said Papa.

Eventually, Daisy got hungry enough to slip through the house in search of smelly socks. She arrived back at the Socksnatchers' hidey-hole with three of them–wouldn't you know?

Abner was pleased to see that Daisy hadn't shut their door tight. He hoped that she'd get yelled at for that. Fat chance!

"We're so proud of you, Daisy," beamed Mama and Papa.

Mama Socksnatcher cooked a big pot of smelly sock soup.
Ummm-m-m! What a fragrance!
They all filled their empty bellies. . .

. . . and crawled into their smelly sock beds.

They were just drifting off into blissful sleep when
the cat burst into the Socksnatchers' hidey-hole!

"DAISY LEFT THE DOOR OPEN!" yelled Abner.
Oh! The TERROR of it all!

Mama Perkins was startled to see the alarmed cat streaking through the house with smelly socks flying in all directions.

Socks continue to disappear at the Perkins' house, but now they think they know who is to blame.

The Socksnatcher family still has a steady supply of smelly socks. They are able to maintain the standard of living to which they have become accustomed.

Everyone lived happily ever after . . . except the cat.